EYEBITER'S REVENGE

JAY BOWER

CHAPTER 1

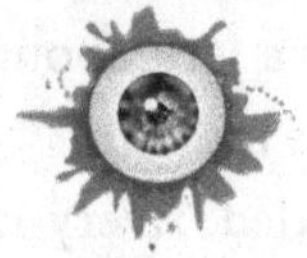

Pete and his four closest friends stood on the concrete steps leading into the old abandoned elementary school, its exterior made of faded brown bricks. A sodium glow from the nearby streetlight cast them in soft shadows. Despite the late summer heat, they were all dressed in long sleeve black shirts with black pants, except Avery, who insisted that her hot pink hairband would not detract from their attempt to remain hidden.

Pete swallowed hard and stared at the entrance to the school. The metal door with glass windows was boarded up with weathered plywood and secured by three locks. It screamed "don't come in," but that was exactly what he had planned.

"You guys ready?" Pete asked.

Their senior year started in two weeks. Pete had taken all summer to build up the courage to break into the school. His friends Avery and Tom were anxious to reveal the ghosts roaming the halls, but Doug and Ray couldn't care less, mostly going along because they had nothing better to do.

"Can we just get on with it?" Ray said. He was the tallest of the group and the oldest, barely missing the cutoff to be in the grade ahead of them when they were in grade school, a fact he reminded them of often. His scraggly beard, that extended an inch from his face, was hidden in shadows and gave him a darker, sinister look.

"You don't have to be a jerk about it," Avery said. "We just got here. Are your panties too tight?"

Tom and Doug chuckled. Avery may have looked like the epitome of the American Girl with her blonde hair and green eyes, but she didn't take shit from anyone. It was one reason Pete became friends with her soon after she arrived in Brownsville with her mother. He laughed to himself at her response to Ray.

"I'm bored," Ray replied. "We're wasting our time. There's no such thing as spirits and ghosts and shit. There's probably some fucking psycho in there ready to gut us."

Avery smiled and stepped closer to Ray. Pete caught a hint of her sweet perfume. Even when breaking into an abandoned school, Avery had to make sure she was presentable.

"Afraid someone might touch you in your funny place?" she asked.

"If you're offering, I'm down with it," he replied.

She huffed and turned away, shifting the strap of the backpack on her shoulder.

All five of them carried a similar pack stuffed with essentials: black candles, lighters, a flashlight, and clothesline.

It was his intent to conjure the spirits within the school and communicate with them. The rumor around town was that the children who died in the shooting were still trapped within the walls of the school. Some claimed the adults were there too, which meant his father might still be there.

None of the five of them brought any fancy cameras to record the session, just the phones in their pockets, not that they were planning to record anything. They weren't trying to make money from the experience, just communicate with those souls trapped inside. And for Pete, it was his last chance to reach out to his father. If the school wasn't scheduled for demo in a few weeks, he doubted he'd have the nerve to break into the place. Haunted houses and ghosts scared the hell out of him.

"Damn, I gotta piss already," Doug said, pushing his glasses back up his nose.

"Fine, we'll get inside so you can break out your dick in the most haunted place in town," Pete replied, eliciting a murmur of laughter from all but Doug.

"Hurry the fuck up," Doug replied.

"Tom," Pete said.

Tom edged closer and pulled a black pry bar from his backpack. He handed it to Pete.

"Thanks, man."

Pete forced it under the bottom padlock and, with two quick yanks, pulled the lock off the weathered board.

"Easy as that," Pete replied. He swallowed hard. There was still time to turn back. He pushed that idea out of his mind. *Dad*, he thought. This might be the last chance.

Doug shifted from one foot to the other. Avery stood with her hands on her hips. Ray and Tom occasionally glanced behind them to make sure no one was watching. It wasn't likely as the school was set back from the main road. Two entrances cut through the trees that surrounded it, out of sight unless you wanted to go back there. Weeds and an unruly underbrush had encroached on the place giving it a more sinister, desolate look. To Pete, it was as if the town had discarded the memory of the tragedy, which meant discarding his father.

With a strained effort, Pete pried open the second lock, letting it fall to the cement steps. When he tried the last one, the lock held firm. The screws holding the latch in place resisted his attempt to snap them. After a couple of tugs, Tom stepped up and grabbed the pry bar with him.

"Ready?" Tom asked. A bead of sweat raced down his cheek.

"Dude, hurry the fuck up," Doug said. "I can feel my bladder ready to burst."

"Why don't you go pee in the grass?" Avery asked. "It's not like there's anyone here."

Doug looked out toward the overgrown weeds that extended from the school to the entrance and cocked his head as though considering it. Pete looked back at the door.

"I'm ready," Pete said to Tom. The two of them pulled, white knuckling it. A moment later, they ripped the screws from the wood with a loud cracking sound. The pry bar flew from their hands and nearly hit Avery in the head.

"What the..." she said, jumping out the way and bumping into Ray. The pry bar clattered on the sidewalk behind them.

"Sorry about that," Tom said. "Pete, let go of it."

"Screw you," Pete said with a smile.

Ray retrieved the bar and handed it to Avery. "You can hit both of them. I won't tell." She looked at it, then shook her head.

"Nah, not yet. But if they do something like that again, I

might." She stuffed the pry bar into her backpack and zipped it shut.

"Open the fucking door," Doug said. He clutched his pants as though pinching a garden hose.

"Ladies and gentlemen. And Ray," Pete said. "I present to you Artemus Ward Elementary School. The most haunted place in Jackson County." With that, he swallowed hard and pulled the creaky door open, stepping inside. The others quickly followed.

CHAPTER 2

Once they were all inside the school, they stood in a tiled hallway covered in dust and debris. Cobwebs clung to the ceiling. Doug pushed past them with his flashlight in hand. The light bounced from one side of the hall to the other, illuminating posters and bulletin boards with hand cut letters and crudely drawn pictures that had curled in the heat over the years. Dust kicked up from the floor, a trail left behind him like footprints on the moon. Halfway down the hall, the beam from his flashlight pointed to his right, and he slipped into the darkness.

"This place is freaky as hell," Ray said. "Stinks, too."

Pete nodded, thinking the same thing. It looked as though the school could've been in use had it not been for the thick layers of dust covering everything. The place had been closed for over fifteen years, and it didn't seem like anyone bothered to clear out the contents. It kinda made sense. Crime scenes were often left untouched.

"How many died here?" Avery asked.

"Twenty-three," Tom replied.

"Including my dad," Pete whispered. Except for Avery, because she only moved to Brownsville four years ago, they all knew someone who died in the shooting. Friends, cousins, people from church. It was devastating.

Pete was there when it happened, but was too young to remember anything. He was in pre-k at the far end of the school. The memories of the tragedy eluded him, blocked by grief and his body's natural response to the shooting. However, he'd seen news stories about the Artemus Ward Shooting to have a sense of the tragedy. Everyone in town knew about it. When a kid shoots up a school in a town of just 8,000 people, it strikes home to everyone.

Pete shined the beam of his flashlight on the walls. A poster admonishing students to "Just Say No" was partially torn. He turned toward the opposite wall and gasped. The others followed the beam.

"Damn," Avery said.

There were three holes in the sea foam green cinder blocks. Bullet holes.

"He just walked in the front door, right?" Ray asked.

Pete nodded slowly. "Yeah, man, there was no security or anything." They stared at the evidence of the violent day in silence, the weight of the moment settling in.

After a minute or so, Avery broke the silence. "Where the fuck is Doug? How long does it take to pee?"

Her words broke the tension, and they left the entrance and headed down the hall toward where Doug left them.

Four light beams bounced within the hall like a wild Hollywood premier. Flashes of broken floor tiles and more bullet holes skipped across Pete's vision. Torn papers and toppled furniture lay strew across the hall beyond the bathroom door where Doug entered.

"Doug, come on, man. Let's get going," Tom said. There was no reply from the bathroom. A light inside indicated he was there, but he didn't say anything.

"Are you playing with yourself?" Avery asked.

"Why, would you like that?" Ray replied.

"Eww, gross. Especially not with you."

Pete and Tom laughed, Ray's face turning bright red.

"Maybe he's taking a shit?" Tom asked. "I need absolute silence for that. The little gopher likes to hide when it's noisy."

"Gopher?" Ray asked.

"Yeah, you know when it pops out and—"

"Dude, we don't need to know," Pete said. "Maybe he's having problems in there. I'll go check."

Pete entered the bathroom and turned to his left, where it opened up to three tall urinals with three stalls next to them. Two sinks lined the opposite wall, rust streaks extending from the faucets to the drains. In the furthest stall is where Doug's flashlight beamed brightly.

"Doug, are you ok man? Do you, like, need toilet paper or something? I might have some tissue in my backpack." Doug didn't reply. Pete stepped closer, following the footprints left in the dust. He crossed the gray-tiled floor and headed straight for the stall.

"Doug, what's going on in there? You aren't jacking off, are you?" He was hoping to elicit laughter, or at least a comment. It was eerily silent, not even the sound of piss hitting the water or grunts from a strained effort.

When Pete reached the stall door, he felt the hairs on his

neck bristle. A cold chill ran across his skin. With the blood rushing in his ears, he pushed open the door.

Doug wasn't there. His backpack lay across the toilet seat and his flashlight was propped against the metal handle behind it. "What the fuck?" he muttered.

"Hey, guys, he's not here!" Pete yelled out. Soon, the others scrambled into the bathroom and stood behind him.

"Look," he said, moving to the side to show the odd tableau.

"Where the hell is he?" Avery asked. "There's only one way in here and none of us saw him leave."

"We would've seen his footprints in the dust, too," Ray said. "Did anyone see a set of prints coming out of the bathroom?" They all shook their heads.

"Something's wrong," Pete said.

"It's the most haunted place in Jackson County, right?" Ray asked. "Maybe a ghost got him." He snickered. Of all of them, Ray was the one most skeptical about the existence of anything paranormal. Pete was pretty sure that the only reason he agreed to come along was the prospect of getting into Avery's pants.

"Eyebiter got him," Tom said.

"We haven't even summoned her," Pete replied.

"Doesn't matter. She's here and we're disturbing her peace. I don't like this at all," Tom said.

"She's not real. It's all made up bullshit," Ray said.

"What about Doug? We gotta find him," Avery said.

"I agree," Pete said. He stared at the flashlight, following the beam to the ceiling, hoping for some sort of clue as to where he disappeared to. Nothing looked out of place. It was as if he had just vanished, but that was impossible. Eyebiter was an even more improbable scenario.

The legend of Eyebiter, a supernatural entity that roamed the streets of Brownsville, was something every child grew up with. Well before the school was shot up, the children of the town were raised to fear this creepy ass woman that fed on kids. It was claimed she had a special affinity for eating their eyes, though Pete never knew a single kid in town that was missing an eye. After the tragedy at the school, the rumors grew to include her taking up residence in the school. Which, of course, was impossible because she would've been at least two hundred years old.

Avery pulled out her phone and pressed a button.

"What are you doing? We don't need the cops here," Pete said. A streak of panic raced up his spine. A moment later, he felt something vibrate in Doug's backpack. He opened it and realized what Avery was doing. It was Doug's phone.

"I really hoped he had it on him. This is messed up," Avery said, ending the call. Pete stared at Doug's phone and wondered his friend had gone. There weren't any missed calls on the screen other than Avery's.

"Oh, gross," Pete said. "Look, there are maggots in here." He opened the backpack wider to show everyone else. Ray let out a soft whistle. Avery feigned vomiting.

"Unless anyone needs to piss, let's get the fuck out of here," Pete said. He stuffed Doug's phone and flashlight into the backpack, then gently nudged Tom and Ray until they all got the hint to leave.

Back out in the hall, Pete ran a hand through his thick brown hair. Cut short on the sides, the volume on top added at least an extra inch to his height, making him appear almost six feet tall.

"If he didn't come this way," Avery said, "then he had to have gone further down the hall." She headed to their right, with Ray right behind her. Tom and Pete followed.

The next door down from the bathroom was wide open. They peeked inside and Pete realized it was an office. A metal desk faced them from the back wall. A toppled lamp and scattered papers lay on top, all covered in thick layers of dust. Right behind the desk on the cinderblock wall was another bullet hole, but this one was surrounded by a large faded brown stain. Pete swallowed. It wasn't brown. It was blood.

"Fuck," he said. "Who was the kid again?"

"Jimmy Lendway," Avery said. "He mentioned Eyebiter, too."

"Shit, he did, didn't he?" Pete replied.

"It was in the journal they found after the shooting," Tom said. "Didn't it say something like 'Eyebiter' made him do it?"

"That's what my mom told me," Avery said. "She studied the case quite a bit after we moved here." Avery's mom was a history professor at the nearby university and had her own supernatural experiences. Pete wasn't surprised that she'd researched local lore as well.

"That's all made up," Ray said. "The kid was fucking crazy, that's all. The Eyebiter story was fake. Someone mentioned it online, and it became part of the stupid lore of a make-believe ghost."

"Why are you so quick to dismiss it?" Avery asked.

Ray extended his hand toward the desk. "A gun and a crazy kid. He was fucked up in the head. He was bullied and didn't have a mommy or daddy to wipe his ass when he needed it."

Pete cleared his throat, trying not to lash out at him.

"Sorry man, I didn't mean anything by it. I know you lost your dad here, and that was awful," Ray said. "But the kid wasn't influenced by anything other than a warped mind and easy access to guns."

"Whatever his real motive was, he ruined a lot of lives," Avery said. She adjusted her pink hair tie, making sure a curl of hair extended perfectly down the side of her face. Pete had been her friend since she moved here, always wanting to make a move but too afraid of rejection. He opted to be "the friend" in hopes that one day she might see him like he saw her. In the dim light given off by their flashlights, she looked beautiful. He turned away and glanced back at the bullet hole.

"He caused a lot of damage," Pete added.

Avery stepped close to him and slipped an arm around him. "Are you sure you want to stay here? We can leave the school. I know this has to be hard for you."

Her calm sincerity caught him off guard. He was so used to her smart-ass comments that he was tongue tied at first. He finally broke through his stupor.

"We can't leave. We have to find Doug."

Avery gave him a gentle squeeze. "Of course," she said, then let go.

"Let's keep going down the hall," Tom said, then led them out of the office.

The musty odor they encountered when they entered the school now carried a hint of something else, something rotten.

"Do you guys smell that?" he asked. "It's like boiled eggs or something."

"I doubt anyone has eaten in here for years," Ray said.

"I know that. It's just…different, I guess," Pete said.

"I bet Eyebiter has eaten something," Avery said.

"Not that shit again," Ray said. "It's not real!"

"Then why did you come with us?" Avery asked, her eyes narrowing and her lips tight.

"I just…I wanted to…you guys are my friends. I didn't want to be left home alone tonight. Besides, it would be my last chance to check out this place." Ray shuffled his feet and avoided looking at Avery. She relaxed her anger and shook her head, as if in disbelief at Ray's words.

"When is demo? It's next week, right?" Pete asked.

"It's supposed to be," Avery said. "But I haven't seen any equipment brought in for it. Maybe they got delayed."

"I don't care what's been planned. We gotta find Doug and get the hell out of here. This was a mistake," Pete said.

"Agreed," Tom added. "I thought we'd get a great story to tell, but this place is creepy as fuck. We shouldn't have come here."

"Doug?" Pete called out. His voice echoed in the hall. "Doug, are you here?"

Ray nudged him. "Dude, not so fucking loud. We'll get caught. I can't have another strike on my record."

"I don't want to get caught in here either, but our friend is missing. We get him and we can go," Pete said.

Avery seemed to agree as she ignored Ray's plea and started calling out for Doug. Tom joined them. Ray grumbled, but then added his voice to the cause.

After several minutes of them calling out for Doug, Avery held out her hand for them to be silent. They listened for his reply, but all Pete could hear was his blood rushing in his ears. The prolonged silence rattled him and the hairs on his arms stood on end, brushing against the inside of his long-sleeved t-shirt.

"We're gonna need to try something else," Pete said. "What if we split up to cover more of the school?"

"I'm not going through here alone," Tom said when they all looked at him. "It's got bad vibes, man."

"We can go in teams of two," Ray said. "I'll go with Avery—"

She cut him off with a laugh. "The fuck you will. I'll go with Pete. You and Tom can go together." The disappointed look on Ray's face was not hard to miss, and Pete forced himself to hold back his laughter.

"Yeah, ok then," Ray said in a low voice.

"Does everyone's phone have service? How much power do you have left?" Pete asked. They all pulled out their phones.

"Yeah, and I'm at ninety-eight percent," Tom said.

"Shit," Ray said. "It works, but I'm down to twelve percent."

Avery shook her head like a disappointed mom. "Maybe charge your shit before you go out. Mine works and I'm at seventy-nine percent."

"I'm good and I'm at eighty-three percent," Pete added. "If you find anything, and I mean anything, call the other group."

"Maybe not Ray, since his phone will probably die out here," Avery said. A smirk crossed her face.

"Fuck, whatever. Let's find Doug and get the fuck out of here," Ray said.

"We'll go to the second floor. You two take this one," Tom added. He nudged Ray's arm and the two of them headed down the hall in search of the stairs, their flashlights bobbing as they walked.

CHAPTER 3

"He really likes you," Pete said to Avery as their friends left.

"I know. But I've never thought of him that way. He's just not my type." She winked, and they crossed the hall to inspect the room.

"Woah," Pete said when his flashlight illuminated a two-foot-tall clown doll that was leaning against a small wooden chair. He took a few deep breaths to calm himself. The clown's once white face was now covered in a grimy patina and the paint on its red lips melted and dripped as though it had a mouth filled with blood. It wore a dark blue outfit with white polka dots that had yellowed over time. It was seated at a small wooden table with three other chairs, one of them toppled over. Stacks of wooden blocks and notecards littered the table.

"Clowns are freaky as fuck," Avery said. She entered the room, giving a wide berth to the creepy clown.

The two of them shined their lights around the room. "Doug? Dude, are you here?" Pete asked. Across the top of the

17

black chalkboard were a series of posters depicting the alphabet and each letter was accompanied by images like animals and objects that started with the same letter. Below the letter 'J,' the chalkboard was damaged. Pete gave it a closer look and realized it was a bullet hole.

"Damn, how many shots did Jimmy get off?" Pete asked.

Avery stopped and looked up as though trying to find the answer. "Hmm, I think it was like fifty or something like that. It was a lot."

Pete shook his head and flashed his light around the room once more. The tiny desks were jumbled up in a heap in the back corner. Papers and books lay strewn about the floor. If Doug was in there, they would've noticed him.

"Next room," Pete said, careful to stay clear of the clown. He had a feeling that if he were close enough, the damn thing might jump out at him. He knew it was impossible, but he'd seen enough movies and read enough books to make him think twice about it.

Someone shouted and the two of them froze. Pete turned to Avery and her eyes widened. As they listened, they heard it again. It was a muffled "Doug" coming from upstairs. Pete let out a breath he'd been holding in, and Avery's eyes relaxed.

"Shit, that scared me," Pete said.

"Same."

The two peered into the next room. It was a small storage room with an old Ricoh copier, yellowed and covered in dust.

"Why do you think they never tore this place down?" Pete asked. "I know they wanted to preserve the scene for evidence, but that was so long ago. Why leave it up? Why leave it like this?"

"My mom told me once that the mayor and city council

wanted to but that some of the parents protested, calling this place sacred or some shit," Avery said.

"Sacred?" He turned from the copier room, clearly empty of people. "I never thought that. I hated that they left it. It's just a constant reminder of what I'll never have."

Avery grabbed his hand and held it close to her chest. "I'm sorry Pete. I know this is hard for you."

Pete's heart raced in his chest. He'd made it to his senior year as a virgin. His hand had never been that close to a girl's boob before and of all girls...Avery? A flood of conflicting thoughts raced through his head. They were shattered when they heard another scream, but this one wasn't like what they heard moments ago. Someone was clearly in pain.

"Doug?" Pete called out, taking his hand back from Avery. "Doug, dude, are you ok?"

"Where's it coming from?" Avery asked.

Pete cocked his head so he could hear it better. "Upstairs, I think."

Another horrific scream and the two of them darted toward the stairs at the end of the hall. They climbed upwards, Pete taking two stairs at a time, until they exited out onto the second floor. It wasn't hard to see where their friends had gone, their footprints easily visible in the thick dust covering the floor though it looked like they went in different directions. A light shone inside a classroom to their right, where the tracks had gone.

"That way," Avery said, following the path on the floor.

A loud, blood-curdling wail came from inside the classroom. When Pete entered the room, he yelled out, and stopped in his tracks, Avery running into him.

"What the fuck?" he said.

Ray was the one yelling, but it wasn't him that worried Pete, it was Tom. Or what was left of him.

Leaning against the metal desk facing the entrance to the classroom was a headless torso. Blood gushed from the neck and oozed down his black shirt. It pooled around his body. One arm hung loose from the body. The only thing holding it in place was a thin strip of flesh.

"Oh my God! What the fuck?" Pete said.

Ray pointed at the body. "His head! Holy shit, where is his head? It's Tom. Fuck. What? Tom?"

Avery screamed when she saw the body. When she did, her flashlight fell to the floor, and the light illuminated something to their left.

"Oh fuck," Pete said. He shined his light on it too. It was Tom's head, his mouth frozen in a surprised expression, but even more sickening than the tendrils that extended outwards from the neck portion like a bloody octopus were his eyes, or lack of. Empty, bloody sockets leaked crimson.

"His eyes!" Avery said. Ray glanced toward Tom's head and when he saw the eyeless face, he bent over to puke. Vomit splashed on the tile floor.

"What happened up here? I thought you two were together?" Pete asked.

Ray answered by puking again, whatever was in his stomach lurching out.

"Eyebiter," Avery said. "It's true. She really exists. She's here."

Ray stood up, wiping his mouth but avoiding looking at Tom, either part of him. "No fucking way is that true."

"Then who did this? Was it you?" Pete asked. A flush of heat cascaded across his cheeks. Could his friend have done this? He didn't want to think it was true, but what else could it be?

Ray took a step closer to him. Pete smelled the rancid vomit on his breath.

"Are you accusing me of something, Pete? Come on out and say it then. You think I did this, don't you?"

Pete took a moment to compose himself. It was difficult to turn his thoughts away from the mangled corpse of his friend next to them, but this needed to be addressed.

"I think you know more than you're saying."

"Fucking idiot. All of you guys are my friends. How could you even assume I had something to do with this?"

"Doug," Avery said, breaking into the conversation. "What about Doug?"

"We hadn't found him. I don't think he was ever up here. Tom mentioned something about the dust not being disturbed when we came up here. Unless there's another way up, I don't see how," Ray said.

"No. What I meant was…could this have been Doug? Do you think he did this to Tom?" Avery asked.

She and Pete turned toward Tom's head. Ray refused to look in that direction.

"Shit, what if he did?" Pete asked. "I mean, I never would've pegged him to do something like this, but I guess it's possible."

"That or Eyebiter," Avery said.

"Or Eyebiter," Pete echoed. A chill ran down his spine. They came here to investigate the legend of Eyebiter, even bringing candles to do a seance to reach out to the malevolent spirit or witch or whatever the fuck the legend was. Could it be their friend they needed to fear instead?

"Fuck, fuck, fuck, fuck," Ray said. "What are we gonna do? We've lost one friend and now…now Tom."

"We need to call the police," Pete said. "We'll catch shit for being in here, but it's better than dying." He tried hard not to think of Tom's last moments and what it was that attacked him, but the freshly mutilated body was hard to ignore. "Let's get out of the room to begin with. I'm starting to feel sick."

The three shuffled into the hallway. A queasiness settled on Pete and a chill ran through him. A vomit and blood scented odor stuck in his nostrils and no matter how much he wiped it with his sleeve, it wouldn't go away.

He pulled out his phone to call the police, dialing 911. Nothing happened. Then he noticed the tiny text at the top of his phone that stated NO SERVICE. "What the hell? I don't have service. What about you two?"

Ray pulled his phone out. "Mine's dead."

Like Tom, Pete thought. And maybe Doug, unless Doug is the one—

"No service for me, either," Avery said.

A knot of worry grew in Pete's gut. This was bad. Something was seriously fucked up about this, and they were all in trouble.

"Then let's get out of here," Ray said.

"But what about Doug?" Avery asked. "He could be trapped in here, too."

"Or he could be the one that killed Tom," Ray countered. "I don't want to be the one to find out."

Avery gave Pete a sad look, her large eyes pleading with him.

"Sorry Avery, Ray's right. The three of us have to leave and let the police handle this. I want to find Doug too, but there's too much at stake here. We don't know if we can trust him."

"But he's our friend," she countered.

"I know." He tried to grab her hand like she did with him, but she pulled away.

"I'm gonna look. Screw it. If he's the killer, I'll take my chances. We always got along pretty good."

Avery brushed past them and headed into the dark hallway, calling out Doug's name. Pete exhaled loudly.

"Man, I'm gonna regret this," he said to Ray, "But I'm gonna stick with her. Come on, we can all stay together."

"It's a dumb fucking idea," Ray said.

"I know, but it's Avery. I'd hate myself if something happened to her."

Ray rolled his eyes and grunted. "Ugh, fuck. Ok, let's go."

CHAPTER 4

Pete and Ray hurried after Avery, following the beam of her flashlight. Pete didn't want to spend any more time in the school. It was a mistake to think they could contact the spirits of the children or even Eyebiter herself. The mistake cost the life of one friend, maybe another. Losing Avery wasn't going to happen if he could help it.

"Avery, wait up," Pete said.

She stopped and glanced over her shoulder, adjusting her pink headband. "You guys didn't leave me. How noble of you. I'm not a stupid damsel in distress. I can handle myself."

"We need to stick together, no matter what. No more splitting up. The three of us will finish checking the school and get the hell out of here. I don't like being around all this death," Pete said.

Even without Tom's mangled body and eyeless head staring at them, Pete wasn't sure coming here was a great idea. To be clear, it was his idea, but once they stepped inside, he'd regretted it.

He'd never been inside the school after they closed it. He

never stepped through the halls of where the terrible tragedy and scene of his father's death occurred. Standing inside the boarded-up school doors brought a dreadful sensation unlike anything he had experienced before. The only reason he didn't turn around to leave was that he was the one who got them all together to begin with. How much shit would they have given him had he backed out of something he organized?

Slowly walking through the second floor of the abandoned school, he regretted not listening to his inner fear. If he had, Doug wouldn't be missing, and Tom would still be alive.

"Did Jimmy ever make it to the second floor?" Ray asked.

"Jimmy?" Pete asked, but then knew it was a stupid question. The gunman. The sick fuck that killed all those kids, along with his dad and four other teachers.

"From what I've read, he didn't get past the first floor because there were plenty of targets," Avery said. "Sorry Pete."

He waved her off. He knew she didn't mean anything by it.

"Why do you ask?" Avery said.

"No reason. The thought just came to me. I wasn't sure about it, that's all."

They poked into a classroom on their left. Unlike the others, it seemed barely touched by time. If it weren't for the layer of dust on everything, Pete thought it would appear like it was still in use. Nothing was toppled over. There were no stray papers lying everywhere. The math questions the teacher was using were still written on the chalkboard, the yellow color barely contrasting with the board.

"It's like a time capsule or something," Pete said. "It's weird. It feels like they just got up, walked out, and never returned. Look," he said, pointing to one of the tiny desks. A lightweight red jacket was draped over the back of the chair, the owner no doubt thinking they were coming back for it someday. They were unaware they'd never return to retrieve it.

"It freaks me out," Avery said. "It's crazy how quickly things change. Like, one minute these kids were bored out of their minds learning about math or vocabulary or whatever and the next, their friends were dead."

"Like Tom," Ray said. "That's fucked up shit."

"That's why we need to find Doug. It's too late for Tom, but we might still have a chance to save Doug," Avery said.

"Assuming he's not the one that did it," Ray added.

"And that," Avery said. "I really don't think it was him. But then again, I have no idea what happened to him. How does someone vanish when they go to the bathroom? We were all there and there was only one way in or out."

"The ceiling tiles weren't touched, either," Pete said. "It's just weird as hell."

They moved on from the pristine classroom and headed across the hall to another. Inside, it was much the same, but a little more chaotic with the trashcan tipped over and one of the desks on its side.

"This place gives me bad vibes," Ray said.

"Same here," Avery added. "The sooner we find Doug, the sooner we can get the hell out of here."

"Hey, the lunchroom is up ahead," Pete said with a touch of giddiness to his voice. The other two stared at him as though he had two heads.

"Sorry, I've never been there, and lunchtime was always my favorite in grade school."

They headed toward the entrance. When they did, Ray entered first. He turned back to the others and froze.

Pete heard something shuffle behind them and spun.

Pointing his flashlight down the hall from where they came, a small cloud of dust hung in the air as though someone had crossed from the left to right, heading into the room opposite of where Tom's body lay.

"What the hell was that?" Pete asked.

"I saw something," Ray said. His flashlight quivered in his hand and the erratic beam of light bounced all around the hallway.

"What was it?" Avery asked.

Pete shuddered. His heart hammered his ribs. All he could think of was Eyebiter, whatever the hell that was.

"I have no idea. But it was someone. I think," Ray said.

"Doug?" Pete shouted. "Doug, dude, is that you?"

"Doug!" Avery and Ray shouted in unison. Then all three of them called him, trying to coax him into joining them.

A moment passed, and they went silent. The dust cloud settled and nothing else stirred.

"Fuck this," Ray said. He then pushed past them and scrambled down the hall, headed for the room where the strange figure entered.

"Ray, no!" Pete shouted. He and Avery froze. Every bit of courage within Pete dissipated as they waited for Ray.

"We should do something," Avery said.

It took all of Pete's will to force his foot to move forward. The second followed. He and Avery slowly crept down the hallway. Ray's light bounced within the room, pointing outward, and then went still, until it finally went out.

CHAPTER 5

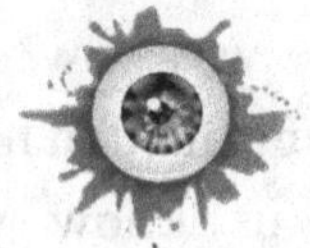

Pete worried that something was wrong. There was too much silence. The air felt dead, as though the violent act from fifteen years before had melded with whatever calamity they were now dealing with and sucked the energy from around them. He didn't want to lose another friend, another life. This building housed far too many deaths already.

Next to him, Avery's breathing broke the silence. She smelled of sweet perfume with a hint of anxiety. Her cheerful pink headband did nothing to lighten the mood. She swallowed hard and turned her large eyes toward him. He fumbled in the darkness until he found her sweaty hand, then held it tight in his, giving it a gentle squeeze. As afraid as he was, he wanted to assure her that it would be alright, even if he didn't fully believe it.

"Ray? Hey man, are you ok?" Pete called out.

"Ray!" Avery added.

Pete wondered what it must have been like to face the gunman, to know that you faced certain death. The kid was only a few years younger than he was now. What possessed him to murder a bunch of innocent kids? Though the reports didn't explicitly state it, he always thought of his dad as a hero in the situation. Jimmy shot his way through the school until he came to Pete's dad and three other teachers. They were found dead as though they'd created a human wall across the hall, blocking the gunman from advancing any further. Was his father as afraid as he was now? He tried to muster the same courage he always imagined in his dad.

"Ray, come on, let us know you're not hurt," Pete called out.

Pete and Avery were within a few feet of the door when the stark silence within the room was cut by loud, piercing cries.

"Ray!" Pete yelled. He moved quickly to the door but was forced to stop before entering when Avery pulled him back.

"Oh God, do you hear that?" she asked.

Ray's horrific cries went quiet. A sickening sound assaulted them. Flesh ripped, wet and meaty. Bones snapped like branches. Ray cried out again.

And then everything went oddly silent.

Pete froze in place, with Avery at his side. Both were breathing heavily. He felt Avery's heartbeat through her hand. Panic raced through Pete. He'd wanted to be brave like he imagined his dad was, but he lacked the conviction. The fleshy sounds replayed in his head, and he closed his eyes to try to force them out.

"Come on. We can't stay out here. We have to look," Avery whispered.

They moved closer to the door. Pete shook. If someone hurt Ray, that person was still in the room. There was only one way in or out and no one had left. They inched closer,

Avery pressing closer to him, her body radiating heat. At another time and in another place, Pete would've enjoyed the touch. But now it was a reminder that they were in a terrible situation.

Side by side, the two of them turned to look into the darkened classroom. Pete shined his flashlight within. A massive streak of blood crossed the floor from the doorway toward the inner darkness. He swallowed hard, fighting back the tears that threatened to fall from his eyes. His breathing grew shallow and quick. He then raised his flashlight and gasped as the cone of light settled on their friend.

"Holy fuck," Pete said. Avery squeaked, words seeming to fail her.

Ray hung from the ceiling, the clothesline from his bag wrapped around both wrists, suspending him from the ceiling in a Christ-like pose from the metal crossbeams of the drop-down ceiling. His head drooped forward, blood spilling out onto the floor.

"Oh my God!" Avery said. She covered her mouth with her hand.

"Is he…is he alive?" Pete asked. He raced to his friend, trying to hoist him off the floor to relieve the pressure of the ropes digging into his flesh. "Avery, help me," he grunted. Ray was barely taller than himself but was far skinnier. Still, Pete struggled to lift him. She joined him and they elevated Ray, the clothesline going slack.

"Guys," Ray mumbled, his voice so unexpected that Pete and Avery both jumped back, letting him fall. He groaned as his arms were pulled taut once more.

"It hurts," Ray said. "I was wrong." His voice was soft and muffled. Ray barely lifted his head, and Avery let out an ear-splitting scream. Both of Ray's eyes were missing, leaving bloody pockets that dripped down his cheeks. Life was rapidly fading from him. The way he spoke and the weakness in his voice told Pete they didn't have much time if they weren't too late already.

"Oh, shit!" Pete said. His stomach twisted and fear bloomed within.

"Who did this?" Avery asked.

"It's true," Ray said. He coughed and spat up blood. He struggled against his bindings, but with his feet unable to reach the floor, he had no leverage. Pete stared in disbelief.

Then he remembered the knife in his backpack. He swung it around and dropped to one knee in one smooth motion.

"Don't worry, man. I'll get you down." Pete's hands shook, and he struggled with the zipper. "Come on, damnit," he grumbled. He finally unzipped the bag and thrust his hand inside. Then he jumped up with the knife in his hand.

Ray's head fell backward, and he let out a loud breath. His chest went still, and his body shifted so that the clothesline tightened against the dead weight. Piss dripped from his pants and a strong stench of shit filled the room.

"He's...dead," Pete said in a quiet voice. Realizing that the killer must still be there, he spun around with the knife held out. Avery shined her light in all directions.

They were alone.

"This can't be real," he whispered. Avery sniffled, and he expected she was crying, but didn't turn to look. His throat went dry, and he couldn't find the words to speak, to express his confusion. Nothing made sense. Everything was screwed up, turned inside out and upside down in a wild, deadly twist that he wasn't ready for.

"Avery, do you see anything in here?" Pete finally said.

"No," she mumbled.

"I don't understand. It was only a minute or two, if that. It would take that long just to string him up. And then his eyes, oh God," Pete said. He turned to the side and, like Ray earlier, vomited all over the floor. The unease in his gut manifested itself into bile and stomach acid, which burned on its way out. It splashed on the blood-stained floor.

Avery pulled him from the room and the smell of death drifted further away. It was too much. They should've left earlier. Now another of their friends was dead. Pete couldn't take his gaze off the darkened room where their friend Ray now hung like an animal ready for processing.

"Eyebiter," Avery said. "Ray was telling us that the story is true. Eyebiter exists and is here. It's stalking us."

They came to the school to find ghosts, the spirits of the innocent whose lives were brutally ripped from them. Pete didn't want to believe that a deadly supernatural being was now hunting them, but the evidence was too much to dispute. The legends had to be true. Wherever Doug was, he would have to fend for himself if he wasn't already dead. Considering what happened to their other two friends, the chances that he was still alive were pretty slim.

"We can't stay," Pete said. "We gotta get the hell out of here."

Avery nodded, the conviction in her manners from earlier all but gone.

"Stick with me and we'll get out together."

"I'm so sorry I made you guys stay," Avery said. "I just thought that we could work together to find Doug. I didn't think he was the one doing this."

"It's not your fault. We made the decision to stay."

Avery gently placed a hand on his shoulder and kissed his cheek. "We get out of this together," she confirmed.

The two of them turned to leave when something shuffled down the hall and into the cafeteria.

"What the fuck was that?" Pete asked, the hairs on his neck stiffening. "Did you see it?"

"Uh huh."

It took Pete a second to decide that whatever it was, he didn't want to find out. There was no sense in risking Avery's life, or his own. They were leaving and getting to some place safe so they could call for help.

CHAPTER 6

Pete folded the knife closed and shoved it in his pocket. He grabbed Avery's hand and led them to the stairwell to their right. Once there, a child screamed from the bottom of the stairs. It sent shivers up Pete's spine.

"What is it?" Avery said, turning to him. Even in the darkened building, he could see the whites of her eyes.

The screams grew louder and more frequent, almost as if there were several children crying out.

"We can't go down there," Pete said, backing away from the stairway. The horrific sounds ended, but their echo remained.

"The cafeteria," Avery replied. "There's another stairway there. It goes down to just in front of the principal's office."

Pete didn't realize there was a second set of stairs. How did Avery know? The school was closed for years before she moved to Brownsville. Now was not the time to question her, not while ghosts or something else were blocking what he thought was their only path of escape.

"But what about that thing we saw go in there?" he asked.

"It's our only way out," Avery said. "We have to try."

Pete ran a hand through his hair again. Every option seemed like a bad one, but they had to choose one.

"Ok," he said. "Let's do it." He patted the knife in his pocket to make sure it was still there. It was the only weapon he had and would have to do if they needed protection.

Shrill laughter bubbled up from the stairwell, setting off alarms within Pete's head. He imagined little children laughing at his distress. Nothing seemed impossible in the abandoned school.

The two of them hurried back the way they came, trampling through their footsteps and heading toward the cafeteria at the end of the hall. One of the two doors was slightly opened, a bloody handprint on the heavy wooden door where someone had pushed their way through.

Pete's heart pounded harder in his chest. Was this really the only way out? Maybe they could escape from a window or something?

At the opposite end of the hall, it sounded like several people were running, as though children were playing in the hall. Pete shined his light in that direction and the beam of light faded before it reached whatever was down there as though the darkness created a shroud that the light couldn't penetrate.

"Now this place is eating light," he said. When Avery scrunched her face at his comment, he nodded down the hall and she noticed it too, her eyes growing wide again.

"That's impossible," she said.

"Everything we've experienced has been impossible, but it keeps happening."

Pete wanted to curl up into a ball and close his eyes until

the horror passed. It was too much, and his sanity was slipping.

When told about how his father was shot in the school and didn't make it, Pete slipped into a similar state of mind. His body shut down. He lay on the floor of his bedroom with a blank stare. It took his grandmother hours to convince him to break out of it and come out of his room. It took another couple of days for him to speak. Had his mother still been alive then, maybe things would've been different. But losing his last parent at such a young age, and in such a brutal manner, broke something inside of him. What was happening now was similar, but with a significant difference.

It may be the same place as his father's tragedy, but this wasn't some deranged kid with a gun. It was an evil force they knew little about that had already murdered two of his friends, if not a third one. Now it had children helping it?

Avery let out a heavy sigh, then gently nudged him into the cafeteria, closing the door behind them.

Inside the large room, darkness prevailed. There were windows along the wall to their right, but they were boarded up years ago. There had to be at least twenty tables, all comically short with attached circular chairs lining both sides of the tables. Two serving windows built into the cinderblock wall ahead of them were closed, shuttered with what looked like small metal garage doors. A metal rolling cart was filled with brown plastic trays. Many had fallen off and lay scattered on the floor. Posters about how milk would do the body good or admonishing students to eat their veggies hung from the walls. Some of them had started to peel away and hung loosely from the tape that had been used years ago, its strength fading.

"Where's the stairway?" Pete asked.

"Back this way," Avery said.

They hurried through the cafeteria toward the wall with the boarded-up windows. As they did, Pete noticed a flickering glow come from a doorway. Because of the angle of the room, he hadn't noticed it earlier.

"Avery, look," he whispered. He pointed his flashlight in that direction, and she gasped when she saw the glow.

"What is it?" she whispered back.

"Do you think there's a fire in there?"

"If there is, maybe we ought to let it burn this place to the ground," Avery said.

"What if Doug is trapped somewhere in here? We can't let him die."

"We're all on our own now. I honestly don't think he's still alive. You've seen what's happened to Tom and Ray. It's safe to assume he was killed as well. Something sinister is happening here, something more terrible than the shooting," Avery said.

"We still can't leave it. If the place is on fire, it'll burn up our friends. The police need to find their bodies so they can go after whoever did that to them," Pete said.

"We both know the cops can't do a damn thing to a witch."

"I'm not convinced it's Eyebiter," Pete said. "Not yet."

Pete stepped closer to the open doorway.

"Pete, what about what's out there? We don't have time for this," Avery said. Pete understood why she'd be worried, but he was compelled to investigate. Something was drawing him to the glow. He had to find out what it was.

When he reached the doorway, his eyes shot wide open. "Avery, come here!" She whimpered but crossed the cafeteria until she stood next to him and peered over his shoulder.

"Holy shit!"
"Doug, are you ok?" Pete asked.

Chapter 7

A mix of relief and fear filled Pete. They'd been looking for their friend ever since they stepped foot into this awful place. Seeing him alive sparked hope that maybe now the three of them could escape…alive. But the hope that so quickly bloomed was just as easily crushed.

Seated in the middle of the barren kitchen was their friend Doug. Stainless steel tables had been pushed to the side, leaving an open space that was about ten feet wide. In the center of that, five black candles burned. A circle had been crudely fashioned with clothesline, with the candles set evenly apart around it. Doug sat cross-legged in the center with his eyes closed, facing them.

His eyes. *Oh no, are they gone?* Pete thought. A shiver ran through him.

"What is this?" Avery asked. "Was he in here the entire time?"

"Wait, look at the floor," Pete said, flashing his light on Doug and the floor around him. In what looked like flour or sand or something similar, lines crossed from one candle to another. "It's a pentagram," Pete said. The candles were placed at five points of the star.

"What the fuck is going on?" Avery asked. "Did he summon the devil?"

Pete wanted to dismiss the notion the moment Avery spoke it, but everything they'd seen that night indicated something odd was happening. Could it have been caused by Doug's dealing in the occult? He had no idea his friend was into that stuff.

"Doug, dude, are you ok? We were worried sick about you. Tom and Ray…they're dead, man. You gotta come with us," Pete said. "We need to get out of here."

Pete froze in his spot, unwilling to cross into the kitchen and come near the demonic symbol. That wasn't their plan when they decided to come into the school in search of ghosts. Honestly, Pete hadn't looked up any kind of ritual. He only chose black candles because it felt like the creepy thing to do, a way for him to amp up the scariness of the place. He never expected they'd have a true, hellish purpose.

"Yeah Doug, come on," Avery added. "We need to get you out of here. Bad shit is going on."

Doug shifted in his spot, the first reaction he made acknowledging their presence. He slowly opened his eyes, and Pete took a step back. Doug's eyes were still there, but they were a milky white, as though someone placed a sheet over them. A faint outline of his iris was visible behind the cloudy haze, but they were far different than ever before.

"Oh, fuck!" Pete said. "Dude, what's wrong with your eyes?"

Doug shifted his head from one side to the other, his neck cracking as he did so. Then he spoke.

"He commands and I obey. He needs his fill. He needs it all. I obey and live."

From behind his back, he pulled out a small cloth bag. Its opening was untied and something dark and stringy hung over the lip like spaghetti. Doug reached in and pulled something out. When he did, Pete felt a sickening feeling tighten in his chest.

It was an eye.

"Joseph commands," Doug said. His voice had taken on a dull monotone quality, nothing like his normal self.

Avery pointed at him. "Where'd…where'd you get that?"

Pete shined his light at the bag. The cloth lip had rolled down, and he realized there were more eyes inside.

"Who the fuck is Joseph? Are those from Tom and Ray?" Pete asked in a shaky voice.

Doug smiled. It was a sickening gesture, something like a madman whose scheme was figured out. A brief flash of a memory tickled Pete's brain. One of the reports about Jimmy, the school shooter, was that he had an eerie grin on his face when he opened fire. Almost every survivor who saw him reported the same thing. A wicked, haunting smile crossed the killer's face. Much like what Pete was seeing on Doug's face.

Doug held out the eyeball. Thin sinewy strands hung from the backside of it, all covered in blood. "This is his. They all belong to him. My life is in Joseph's hands. He will be set free. The sacrifices are all for him. Blood and death. Eyes. All the eyes. For him."

"You aren't making any sense," Avery said. "Joseph? We don't know anyone by that name. Doug, please, snap out of it. We can all get out of here alive."

Something thudded against the doors to the cafeteria. The

sudden disturbance made Pete jump. He turned that way but didn't see anything.

"It's gotta be those things from the stairs," he said. A sudden urge to evacuate his bowels struck him and he fought hard to keep everything intact.

"Doug, what the hell, man? How'd you get in here? We lost you in the bathroom and never saw you leave," Pete said. "We can talk about that later, though. We have to get the hell out of here. Something is coming after us, and I don't think they're friendly."

The grin on Doug's face grew impossibly wider, his lips stretching to their limits. It made Pete shudder.

"Joseph," Doug said. "Joseph is back."

"Who is that?" Avery asked. She tilted her head upwards as though in deep thought. No doubt she'd scoured the local legends with her mom, the history professor. Pete tried to connect the name as well. The legend of Eyebiter was that she was a woman named Sarah, a distant relative of Nathaniel Browne, the founder of Brownsville. But who was Joseph? The only Joseph he knew was his father, but he went by Joe, and he'd been dead for fifteen years.

Doug moaned, stealing their attention. His eyes fluttered. The candles flickered.

"I don't like this," Avery said.

"Doug, come on, snap out of it. Whatever is going on, we can get help for you," Pete said.

Something pounded on the cafeteria door again and Pete spun around. The doors were slowly creaking open, but from where they stood, he couldn't see what it was. Haunting giggles followed. Pete dropped his flashlight, and the light winked out. He snatched it off the floor and shook it, but the light was dead.

"Damn it," he mumbled.

Doug let out a demonic howl. It was so sudden and so powerful that Pete clapped his hands against his ears to block out the sound, though it didn't help much. Avery had done the same.

"He's lost," she said, indicating Doug. "Whatever this thing is, it has him in its grips. We have to leave him behind. We gotta save ourselves."

The decision paralyzed Pete. Doug was their friend. How could he condemn him to his death?

Doug groaned again, the voice so deep and unlike him that it sounded like it came from someone else. The cafeteria door creaked again. Despite his misgivings, Pete's decision was made for him.

"Sorry Doug. I don't know what happened to you, but we can't do anything for you." It stung like hell, but Avery was right. They had to leave or face horrific consequences like Tom and Ray.

"Let's get to the stairs," Pete said. They rushed to the open doorway, and he looked back at his friend, who sat still in the diabolical circle, his white eyes fluttering in the candlelight.

They stepped into the cafeteria and, half expecting to find a demon or wicked creature, they found nothing. Avery scanned the area with her flashlight, and it was empty.

"I don't like this," Pete said. "We both heard it, right?"

"Yeah. It's like those dead children are after us."

"Fuck it, we aren't waiting around," Pete said. He nudged her toward the stairs, and they ran across the room with the tiny tables, avoiding them and crossing aisles when one was in their way. When they got to the stairwell, Doug let loose a bloodcurdling scream.

"Oh no!" Pete said. He looked back and didn't see anything other than shadows moving in the candlelight. The angle wasn't good, and he couldn't see what exactly was going on inside the kitchen.

"Doug!" Avery screamed.

Doug howled again, pleading for mercy.

"Please don't!" he screamed. "I'm yours!" Then his pitch rose higher, his screams more agonizing. It was punctuated by a loud plop. The visual in Pete's head made him sick. He couldn't see what happened, but his imagination ran wild.

"He killed him," Avery said. "Whoever this 'Joseph' person is killed Doug, even though he helped him."

Pete fought back the tears and turned toward the stairs. "We can't stay," he mumbled, then headed downstairs.

CHAPTER 8

When Pete and Avery stepped out into the darkness of the first floor, a cold sensation made his skin prickle. Doug had fallen silent, but a heavy thud upstairs was followed by what sounded like something being dragged across the floor.

"Which way?" he asked. He was turned around and didn't know what hall they were in or where the exit was. The emergency exits no longer illuminated after years of neglect.

They were at a t-shaped crossing with one hall extending straight ahead. Avery used her flashlight to look down all three paths. Above them, the unmistakable sound of something being dragged grew louder, closer. Pete was ready to dart down any of the halls, just so long as it got them away from that sound.

Then it stopped.

Pete cocked his head. A heavy splat followed, spraying them both with a hot liquid. He and Avery jumped and spun around. When her flashlight shone on the source of the awful sound, Pete screamed.

It was Doug. Or rather, what was left of him. His body had been shredded. Long ribbons of flesh hung loose from his arms. The way his body fell from the second floor, they extended outwards like bloodied tendrils. His head had cracked open, and his face was turned toward them. Gray matter spilled out onto the floor.

"His eyes," Avery said. "Fuck, he got his eyes."

Just like their other two friends, Doug's eyes were plucked out. Pete imagined they were added to the bag with the others, but for what purpose? A collection of stolen eyes held no value. At least, not that he knew. To one called Eyebiter, maybe they held a sacred meaning.

Pete stumbled backwards and, without waiting for Avery, ran down a hall. He had no idea which one. It was just a means to get away from the madness. He screamed the entire time, letting loose the terror that had been building within him. Fuck Eyebiter. Screw the wicked man, or whatever the fuck it was. He couldn't stay silent any longer. Something snapped inside of him, and he was powerless to stop it.

Avery called to him, but it was like he was in a dream and the voice was distant and disembodied.

Pete faced the need of the hall and stopped, his hands on his knees. The terror of the night raced through his mind, and he fought hard to push it back.

A light bobbed closer to him, and he shielded his eyes from its brightness.

"Sorry, I didn't mean to do that," Avery said. She turned her light toward the floor. "Pete, don't run off like that. Not without me. Hold it together so we can get out of this alive."

"Doug," he said between breaths. "He just tossed him over

the stairs like he was nothing. I can't take this anymore. It's too much."

"We can make it out, but only if we stick together. We can do this," Avery said.

Pete took a few calming breaths.

He focused on her words, trying to maintain his composure. It wasn't like him to snap like that. There was just too much going on, and when Doug was tossed from the second floor, he couldn't hold it in any longer. Avery would need him to maintain his sanity, and he clung to that thought. It was tenuous, but it was enough to push away the fear, if only for a moment. She was right. Together, they could figure out how to get the hell out of that place and never turn back.

"The bad news is that you went down the wrong hall. This one is a dead end," Avery said. "That's how Jimmy was able to kill so many. They ran this way and didn't have any way to escape."

She did a quick check of the walls with her flashlight and the cinderblocks were littered with pockmarks, the remnants of the gunman's rampage.

Pete swallowed hard. "This," he began in a weak voice, "this is where my dad died."

He knew little of the events of that day, but the one thing he'd been told over and over again was that his father led a class down this hall and all but one of them died. He was criticized in the newspapers and vilified for his actions, with some people even accusing him of leading them to their deaths on purpose. It was too much for Pete to bear at the time and soon afterwards, he was in therapy five days a week instead of two.

"Oh damn, it is," Avery said. "This must be awful." Avery

wrapped an arm around him and pulled him close, offering her best sympathetic hug.

A loud screech echoed through the school. The two of them clutched each other and faced down the hall.

"Avery, we're gonna have to go that way, aren't we?"

"It's the way out. We're dead if we stay here."

The screech intensified, growing darker and undulating in pitch.

"Shut up!" Avery said.

Pete clutched her head, covering her ears with his arms. But that meant he was forced to listen to the hellish sound, and it made his blood run cold.

The screams stopped, and he let Avery go. She was breathing heavily, as he was.

"Ready? Tell me which way to go. I'll lead. I couldn't stand myself if something bad happened to you," Pete said, mustering the courage he'd lost earlier.

"Back. We go back to the intersection and follow the hall directly across from the stairs. At the end of that, turn left and the entrance should be there. Unless I have my bearings all screwed up."

Pete pulled the knife from his pocket. The small blade wouldn't do much damage, but it gave him a sense of security he sorely needed at that moment.

"Shine the light ahead of us. We'll move slowly."

Avery did as he asked, and then he walked ahead.

The terrible screams stopped; their echo left ringing in Pete's ears.

"Thank God," Avery said. "I couldn't think with that going on. Pete, if we don't make it out of here, I want you to know that I really like you. I never realized how much until tonight."

He stopped. That was not what he expected to hear. "Umm, so I, uh…thank you." He felt his cheeks flush.

Slowly, they worked their way back to the intersection, keeping some distance away from the stairwell. Avery's flashlight landed on Doug's broken body and she let out a squeak. They pushed themselves against the wall opposite the stairs. Pete kept his hand on the rough block walls, feeling the grooves within. At one point, his finger slid into a jagged hole. Without looking at it, he knew it was a bullet hole. His heart sank. Was it done before or after his father was killed? To be so close to where he was murdered unsettled him, and he yanked his hand free of the wall.

They got to the intersection of the halls, and Avery shined her light ahead of them.

"I don't see anyone," she said.

"Let's get out," Pete answered. His overworked mind and raw nerves had had enough of the school. It was a mistake to have come here.

They entered the hall and moved slowly. There was still something lurking in the school, and it maimed and killed their friends.

Halfway toward the exit, a deep and menacing growl echoed in the darkness. At first, Pete thought it was a dog, like a Rottweiler or a pit bull.

"Avery, what is that?"

She swung her flashlight around, searching the shadows for the source of the sound. "I don't know. I think it's coming from that classroom." Her flashlight landed on an open door across the hall from them.

The sinister growl continued, and Pete felt a chill race down his spine. "Do you think that's her?" He didn't need to say the name. He knew Avery would know exactly who he meant.

Avery ran her free hand over her headband, her eyes darting back and forth from the room to the exit. "Maybe?"

"We need to run for it. We're almost to the door," Pete said.

The growl turned into a wild, high-pitched shriek. Pete shuffled away, his heart racing and his eyes growing larger.

The darkness in the hall grew darker, a phenomenon Pete didn't think was possible. The air suddenly turned frigid, and his flesh prickled.

"Avery, it's her," he whispered, afraid to speak any louder for fear of capturing Eyebiter's attention.

Avery lifted her flashlight, so the beam pointed at the sudden darkness blocking the hall from where they came.

A figure shrouded in shadows stood with its head nearly touching the ceiling. It covered its face with arms dripping in thick strands of shadow, obscuring its face. Pete froze, and his bladder almost gave out.

"What is that? Is that…"

Avery clung to him, her earlier bravado slipping away in the presence of the malevolent creature.

A low growl escaped the thing, and then it dropped its arms. The shadow dissipated from around it and it shrunk in size. What was left made Pete gasp. Words failed him, but deep inside, he screamed. It was impossible.

It was his dad.

CHAPTER 9

Pete was only three when he was killed in the shooting, but he'd thumbed through photo albums for hours at a time, attempting to connect with a man he barely knew. It had only been the two of them since his mother's unexpected death when he was just a baby. Memories of his dad tucking him into bed were all that he had and even then he wasn't sure those were real or manufactured by a traumatized mind.

But the man standing in the hall was the man from the photos, though with significant physical differences. He had no doubt it was his father, Joseph Speight.

"What's wrong, son?" he asked. His voice sent chills through him. He'd heard recordings before, but there was always a metallic timbre present. His words now sounded smooth and dark. He held something in his hands, but he couldn't tell what it was.

Pete's words refused to form, the shock of the moment tightening his throat.

The person before him was an emaciated version of his father. Taught, ashen skin was draped over his skeleton. His thin lips were cracked. His hair was nearly gone, exposing a bone white skull. He wore tattered clothes, his shirt in ribbons and his pants shredded. But despite all the changes, it was something in his eyes that reminded Pete of the memories he had of his father. There was no doubt that this creature staring at him was his dad.

"Son," the eerie man said. Shadows drifted from him in curls of smoke. Avery's shaky flashlight made them even more menacing. "It has been so long. You've grown into a fine young man."

The man, his dad, shuffled closer, shambling across the tile floor unsettling the dust underneath him.

"This isn't real," Pete whispered, words finally escaping his lips. It was impossible. How could his father be here?

He smiled wide, his black pit of a mouth growing larger and his lips cracking worse than before. "Come now, is that how you greet your father?"

"You're not his father!" Avery yelled. Pete glanced at her and then back at the creature.

"Your eyes will be a delight," his father said.

Pete's legs grew weak, and he almost fell down. "Eyes?" he asked.

His father cackled. It was a wicked sound that dripped with evil. "My son, isn't that why you came back? To see me, to see the one you call...Eyebiter."

Pete stumbled backwards. Avery grabbed his arm and held tight.

"No," he said. "No, it can't be true. You aren't...no, please dad, tell me it's not true."

"That's not your father," Avery muttered. "Don't listen to his lies."

Pete was thrown into confusion. All the legends said Eyebiter was a woman, a witch from the earliest days of the settlement. How could this thing in front of him be the legend and his dad? It was impossible.

"You will understand the truth, but that will be the last thing you do," his father said. He held out what was in his boney hand. A brown cloth bag, the one Doug had in the cafeteria. The one filled with eyes.

"I hated these little children," his father said, extending his sickly looking arms, indicating the school. His shirt hung from his skeletal frame. "They drained my energy, made me weak, but I soon discovered they could help me."

Help you? Pete thought. He wasn't sure he wanted to know.

"Jimmy did as I commanded, but he was reckless. He destroyed the source of my strength like a brute. The eyes must be harvested with their souls attached. His methods were too quick, too final for me to extract what I needed. I asked him to maim, but the killing frenzy took over. When I brought him more children, he turned the gun on me." His father inhaled deeply, continuing his awful speech.

"Ever since that day, I've waited for freedom. My spirit lives within these walls, but I need to escape. In death, the children taunt me worse than in life. Their sickening laughter reminds me how much I loathe them. But these," he said, holding up the bag, "these are what bring me life. These will break the bonds which tie me here. And Doug was more than eager to fulfill my needs." He poked into the bag and plucked out an eye, thin bloody strands dangling from it. He inspected it like he was choosing a diamond. "His gift," he said, then held the eye to his lips. And bit.

It popped like an overripe grape. Blood and gore dripped

down his chin. He chewed with his eyes closed, his head back in ecstasy. Slowly, his jaw moved as he savored the soft bite. He slurped up the thin strand connected to the piece he bit off and licked his dry lips. He took a couple deep breaths and let out a soft moan.

"Have you ever tasted the soul of another?" he finally asked.

Pete was shaken to his core. His feet refused to move, frozen in place. Was that truly his father and did he just eat Doug's eye?

His father poked the other half of the bloody eyeball into his mouth and gazed at Pete as he chewed with his mouth partially open like it was scalding hot and he needed relief.

"The final bite is always the best," he said.

Pete's stomach twisted into knots.

"Fucking gross," Avery said.

"But oh, so necessary, little one," he said.

Avery grabbed Pete's arm and pulled him away from his father, Joseph. "We have to get out of here!"

Pete's fear intensified as his father's face twisted and contorted in on itself. Deep fissures creased his flesh and peeled back, his thin skin tearing away. He plucked another eye from the bag and popped it into his mouth, chewing loudly on the bloody orb. It splashed on his teeth, and they dripped a thick crimson liquid. But as he did so, his face returned, and the deep gashes closed on itself.

"He's healing with each bite," Pete said. None of it made sense. How could the spirit of his dad be doing all this?

Avery let out a whimper. "This really is the witch or...or... something."

Joseph raised a boney finger at her. "You would do well to

join us. Your mother knows all too well the dealings with the dark one. Come, join her."

Pete faced Avery; her eyes bulged.

"No! Please don't. It's not…it's not true!"

"Avery, what does he mean?"

She shook her head, her hand covering her mouth.

Pete spun her around and pulled her along. He wasn't staying one more second in this place. Father or not, the creature facing them was dark and disturbing. "Come on, let's go!"

CHAPTER 10

They raced away from Joseph. Pete glanced back, but with the light gone, he saw nothing but an open maw of darkness. The thing that claimed to be his father could be anywhere behind them.

A rumbling growl echoed in the hall. Pete's heart thumped harder, his adrenaline kicking in, and his muscles screamed from exertion.

They made it near the end of the hall where the final corridor crossed, revealing the exit to their left. He had no idea where his father had gone to, but Pete was thankful for finding their way out. He yanked Avery in that direction, and she was ripped from his arms.

"No!"

Avery's ear-splitting scream jolted him. She was pulled back into the darkness, and she dropped her flashlight. It clattered on the tile. In a sliver of light, he caught a glimpse of a black shadow escaping into the nearby classroom. Which is also where Avery's scream came from.

Pete snatched the flashlight from the floor. He had to

hurry. If his father was as quick as he thought he was based on what he'd done to Tom and Ray, he didn't have a second to spare. He needed to save Avery from whatever fate awaited her. It was not supposed to be like this. They were only here to commune with the dead, not die themselves.

Pete ran to the room and lunged inside.

The flashlight shined on a frightened Avery. She floated in front of the desk at the back of the room with thin wisps of black shadow swirling around her like living bindings. His father was next to her. A dusty wooden nameplate on the desk had the name "Mr. Speight" engraved on it. Pete's eyes grew large.

"This was your class."

He was too young to remember where his father's classroom was. Because he was killed further back in the school, he always associated his class with being back that way. It was only now that he remembered the rumors about his father's actions in the shooting, despite his death at the hands of the killer.

The news reported he assisted Jimmy, that he somehow let him in the building, but he always thought that was crazy. He often wondered why his father would let him in to kill all the kids. It never added up but was a constant source of embarrassment for him. Until now. Until the words his father shared moments earlier shattered his hero worship.

"This was your class," he repeated. "Why?"

His father grinned and stepped closer to Avery. His friend didn't seem like she could speak, but her wild eyes and convulsions gave away how frightened she was.

"I never wanted children. You were your mother's idea. When she selfishly died, leaving you with me, I burned with a hate so deep. Working around children reinforced my disgust with you."

Pete's eyes filled with hot tears. How could his father be saying such awful things?

"Then it became all about the eyes."

A deep gash opened on his father's face again, but this one wept black blood. Things crawled out of it, wiggling out of the wound, and landing on the floor. Another gash crossed his forehead and black worms worked their way out from inside and crawled down his nose. They fell to the floor. When he spoke, more of them fell from his face.

"I wanted to be rid of you long ago, but I couldn't bring myself to do it. Not personally. That's where Jimmy came in, but he failed me and when I tried to stop him, he turned it on me."

He smiled, more worms falling from his face. Then he produced the bag of eyes that was sitting on the desk and plucked out an eye. He set the bag back down and slowly savored an eye, slurping on the nerve attached to it.

"You brought him in…to kill me?" Pete said. The revelation shook him to his core. How evil was he? All those kids died because he wanted his own son dead, and he was incapable of doing it himself. Pete's face darkened, and he glared at him. Hate boiled within. Ever since his death, he had a longing for him, a deep chasm inside his soul that could only be filled with his love, but this? He'd never have guessed this.

His father smiled, then bit down, severing the orb in his mouth. Pete heard a soft pop through his closed lips as he chewed. The moment he did, the cuts on his face closed up and he was healed from his grotesque wounds.

Avery struggled against her shadowy bonds, but couldn't

escape from the force holding her. Pete's stomach was doing flips, the grossness of his father eating an eye and the truth of his revelation unsettling him.

How was he going to stop him? If this was an evil spirit or a witch or something like that, how could he do anything to him?

His father placed a gnarled hand over Avery's face. Avery opened her mouth to scream, and nothing came out, her face a mask of pure terror. His father dug his black nails into the eye socket on Avery's right side.

Pete lunged forward, but his father was too quick. He heard the sound of Avery's eye plucked from her skull, a disgusting, wet, sucking sound. Pete slammed into Avery. He hadn't expected his father to let her go, but he released the bond and the two of them tumbled onto the desk. Pete fell face down and stared at the bag with the remaining eyes. The idea struck him like lightning. The eyes. He said it was all about the eyes.

Avery cried out and clutched her now empty eye socket. Sympathy welled up inside Pete, but the time to console her wasn't now. Not when he had someone to stop.

He grabbed the bag and the thin wooden nameplate from the desk, spinning around to face his father. If these are what gave him strength, then destroying them was the only way he could think of to stop him.

CHAPTER 11

Pete's father was inches from him and held out Avery's bloody eye, the green iris looking back at him from between her fingers. A storm of anger and confusion raged within Pete. Facing the monster that was his father shook him to the core.

"Recognize this one?" his father said. A stench of rot and decay invaded Pete's nostrils and his stomach lurched. He held his breath, trying to avoid tasting it.

His father backhanded him, the blow coming unexpectedly. Pete flew across the room and the bag slammed against the wall, the eyes inside falling out. The wooden nameplate flew in the opposite direction.

"My eyes!" his father screamed. Before he ate Avery's eye, he dove to the floor and felt through the dust for his prized possessions.

Pete stood on shaky legs. Avery was on her knees with her face in her hand. The faint light from the fallen flashlight illuminated angry streaks of blood that raced down her arms, evidence of her missing eye.

Fueled by rage, Pete lunged at his father. He slammed into his corporeal body, the physicalness of him a shocking surprise. The two of them hit the wall and Pete thrashed, trying to disengage himself. His hand slammed down on something wet. It crushed underneath the force and his hand was covered in a thick, sticky substance.

His father roared. "No!" he bellowed. Rising up on his haunches, he flung out his hands and tried to grab Pete. His nails scraped Pete's skin. The wounds he left were hot and stung like a thousand bees.

Pete fought through the agonizing pain to search for the other eyes. With Avery's eye, he expected there should be three left.

His father flung his hand out and Pete was tossed back several feet, even though he never touched him. Pete crumpled to the floor and slowly uncurled himself, ready to destroy the eyes. In the darkness, he just barely saw his father shove an eye into his mouth and eat, a deep groan escaping from him.

Two more. He had to destroy the last two if he had any chance of escaping.

His father cackled and rose to his full height. Pete flashed the light on him. With a wicked grin, his father held out a skeletal hand with two eyes in his palm, one brown and one green. *Avery's eye*, Pete thought.

"You were an embarrassment once. You're not any better now. At least you will serve a purpose before you die." His father lifted one of the eyes to his mouth, but Avery had recovered. Pete's dad didn't see the girl as she dove into him. The force of the impact made him drop one of the eyes and reflexively crush the other as he braced himself.

Avery screamed wildly. Pete's dad howled at the loss of his

precious stolen eye. The two of them struggled on the floor, with Pete's father threatening to eat Avery's remaining eye right out of her skull.

Pete had to do something. There was no way he'd let his father kill Avery. If it was the last thing he did, he'd save his friend. This was not her fight. It was between him and his dad.

That's when he spotted the last eye. It had rolled against the wall and was covered in dust. A glimmer barely caught his attention in the faint light, but he knew what it was.

Hurrying toward it, he snatched it from the floor and held it up.

"Joseph!" he yelled, ditching the formality and refusing to call the monster his father. "Let her go."

Avery scooted away from Joseph, who was distracted by the appearance of the eye.

"Give it to me," he snarled. "You don't know what kind of powers you are dealing with."

Pete held the sticky orb between his thumb and forefinger. For a second, he wondered which one of his dead friends it belonged to. If he ever escaped this madness, he vowed to make sure their memories were never forgotten.

"Leave us. Go back to wherever the hell you came from," Pete said.

Joseph rose to his full height. He snarled, then a crack opened on his cheek. Maggots and worms wriggled their way out. He tried to cover it up with his hand, but the insects still squirmed through his thin fingers.

"Give that to me!"

"You need the power, don't you?" Pete asked. All the rumors of an eye eating witch were true, and much to his horror, they involved his own father, this thing in front of him named Joseph.

Flashes of gunfire erupted in his head. Screams. Children crying. People shouting. Bullets ricocheting off the concrete. Memories he hadn't accessed in years assaulted him.

Across the room, Joseph grinned. Worms crawled in and out of his mouth. Maggots inched down his cheeks. More cuts erupted on his flesh, which had now taken on an even more pale gray hue.

"Give in to the fear. Remember your past. Let go of the present and abandon hope," Joseph said.

"Fuck you," Pete said. Against the backdrop of his past racing through his head, he narrowed his eyes and glared at him. "Fuck you and your evil ways." He then wrapped his hand around the last eye and squeezed.

Joseph wailed. It was an awful, demonic sound.

The eyeball popped and gushed into Pete's hand. It felt like a ball of puss had burst. Like a giant blister filled with sickening fluids. The inside of the eye coated his hand in a sticky substance.

Joseph's face turned upwards. Worms and centipedes and maggots crawled out of his skin. His head shook violently, and the creatures sprayed all over the room. Pete covered his face with an arm. He felt tiny things fling against him and he backed up several steps.

"Avery!" he called out. He felt a tug on his shirt, and he turned to the side. It was her. He wrapped an arm around her and the two of them clung to each other as Joseph continued to howl and cry out.

More of the bugs escaped his flesh. They clung to Pete. Frantically, he brushed them off as though they might infect him with Joseph's evilness. Whatever ate away at Joseph's decency would never infect him. The wickedness would end with him.

Joseph screamed again. Pete and Avery were both locked on to him, their eyes unable to turn away.

The shadows that had circled him started moving like a violent storm. They swirled around his head until they closed like a noose around his neck. Then the shadows crept upwards, snakelike, slithering up his neck and chin. It split into several tendrils, each one stabbing at the wounds on his face. Another strand broke free and slid into his nostril. His eyes grew large. There was a slight pause. An unsettling silence followed.

Joseph grinned. The worms in his mouth dangled from his teeth.

"It's not over," he hissed.

Then the shadow shoved itself into his mouth. His face expanded like a wicked balloon. Veins bulged; their dark lines visible under his translucent flesh. His wounds wept blood, the insects no longer pouring out. Then, just as Pete thought it couldn't get any worse, Joseph's head exploded.

Black blood splashed the wall behind him. It sprayed Pete and Avery. Its rank odor was like nothing he'd ever experienced.

While the two of them watched, the black shadow consumed Joseph's body, devouring it. He screamed a high-pitched wail. Both Pete and Avery covered their ears until the horrific cries ceased.

Within minutes, the room fell silent.

Blood rushed in Pete's ears. Avery's breathing grew shallower, and she whimpered. He turned the light on her.

It took everything he had not to jump away in revulsion. A couple maggots crawled around her empty eye socket, feasting on the fresh blood. Without thinking, he brushed them away, and she yelled as he touched exposed nerves.

"Maggots," he said, trying to explain his action. He thought he saw another one deeper within, but he was not about to touch it. Hopefully, she'd feel it and take it out herself.

"We have to go," he finally said, recovering from the moment. "Can you make it out?"

Avery nodded without replying. She covered her exposed eye socket with one hand, and he led her out of the room. At the door, he glanced back at the empty room. All that was left of Joseph was the stain on the wall and the wooden nameplate. He grunted and then led Avery out of the school.

Chapter 12

Pete tapped his fingers gently on the wooden table. He had asked Avery to meet him at Coffee Haven, their local coffee shop. She had yet to arrive, and the waiting was eating at him. They hadn't spoken in days, and she wouldn't text him back until after the fifth try, when she finally relented and agreed to meet.

When she arrived, he grimaced at her. She wore a black eyepatch over her one eye. He imagined it hurt like hell and a touch of guilt settled within him. Without his insistence on finding ghosts, she might still have an eye. And his friends might still be alive.

"Hey," he said, breaking from his thoughts.

"Hi," she replied in a neutral tone.

"You want any coffee?" he asked.

She shook her head. "No, I'm fine."

He gestured with a hand for her to sit. They were at the back of the shop, far from the door. Black and white photos of bags filled with coffee adorned the wooden slat walls. Pete waited for an older couple next to them to leave before speaking.

"Are you ok? Have you spoken to the police?"

She nodded. "I said what we agreed on."

When the police questioned Pete and Avery about the incident, they both agreed to blame it on their friend, Doug. No one would believe they'd actually come up against the legend known as Eyebiter, so they did the only thing they could think of.

Neither one of them fully understood how Doug was involved and how he escaped the bathroom that night, but after all they'd seen and been through, both could believe anything.

"Good. I hate that we had to, but..." He trailed off. It didn't need to be said aloud.

Avery barely looked at him with her good eye, instead her focus was on the table, as though she were inspecting it.

"Speak to me," Pete said in a soft voice. "I want to help. I know you've been through hell, and not just with, well, you know who."

Avery had gone missing not long after her and her mother moved to town and her mother had a mental breakdown, blaming spirits or wraiths. She didn't deserve another tragedy in her life, and it broke his heart that she'd been put through another terrible trial.

"It's fine, I promise."

"When do you get your eye?"

His question invoked a slight smile on her face, the first sign of life yet. "In two weeks. The doctor said it'll take me some time to adjust to it, but after a while, I won't know it's there."

"How's your vision?"

"It still throws me off. My balance is all out of whack, but I manage."

"Avery, I'm so sorry this happened to you. It was me he was after. I know that now. I wish we'd never have gone there that night. It was dumb."

She blinked and gazed into his eyes with her one remaining eye. "I'm not sorry."

"What?"

"I mean it. I'm not sorry we went."

"Avery!"

"Things happen for a reason. I'm not the same anymore, and I'm thankful for that."

Pete didn't know that to say. This was not what he expected. Sleep eluded him the past few nights, haunted by the memories of that night and the horrible deaths of his friends.

As he stared at her, a small maggot crawled out from under her eyepatch. She noticed it, plucked it off of her skin, and tossed it to the floor.

"If that's all you have to say, then I think I need to go," Avery said. She stood, and Pete jumped to his feet.

"Avery?"

She smiled, and when she did, it was like looking at Joseph. He couldn't explain it, but there was something in the way her lips curled back. A sickening feeling settled in his gut.

"See you around," she said, then tiptoed out of the shop. A shiver ran up Pete's spine. Something was wrong with Avery, and he felt sure Joseph was behind it. The thought slammed into his mind like a lightning bolt.

"Oh no," he whispered. He covered his mouth with his hand, the truth dawning on him.

Eyebiter was still alive, and now he lived in Avery.

ABOUT THE STORY

This story was originally published in *The Conservator's Collection: Derelict* which was a project started after meeting both John Lynch and John Durgin at Authorcon 2 in Williamsburg, VA in 2023. Lynch had a table right outside of my room and all weekend long we chatted about books and horror and everything else. I met Durgin but we didn't get a chance to talk much since he was in another section of the event, but I did make it a point to connect with him because I was so impressed with his talent.

After leaving, I stayed in contact with Lynch through texting and I was itching to do some type of collaborate project with him. I took a chance and asked if he'd like to work together. He was onboard right away. In our discussions, we decided we needed a third author to join our madness and both of us immediately suggested to the other that we'd love to work with John Durgin. We reached out and he joined without hesitation.

Working with those two has been amazing. Both Durgin and Lynch work hard on their craft while building a name for themselves. Though I've been publishing longer than both of them, I've learned a ton from our daily chats. I'm so thankful for their insights and I'm honored to call them friends.

I must mention Joe Ripple, Brian Keene, and all of the Scares That Care family for hosting AuthorCon. It's an event that raises money for charity and in turn, is the premier horror author event in the world! Without the opportunity to attend AuthorCon, this story might never have existed.

I'd like to thank Candace Nola, a badass author in her own right, for editing this book and helping my story shine.

MIBLArt created the cover for this stand-alone version and I'm thankful for their work. They've created several covers for me and I highly recommend them.

I'd like to thank Daydream Studio for the custom interior artwork. The Eyebiter turned out so good!

My readers have been truly amazing, and I can't thank them enough for their support, their love, and their friendship. Most of them reside within Bower's Basement of Humanity and to all the Cellar Dwellers out there, YOU are the best! None of this happens without you. Thank you for sticking by me and being such vocal proponents of my work.

In January of 2024, I started a Patreon and was overwhelmed by the generous support from so many of you. I want to give a personal thanks to Megan Stockton, Candace Nola, Deven VanKirk, Lisa Breanne, Jason Artz, Dottie Sargent, and Teresa Howell. I am deeply indebted to you and appreciate your massive support.

Finally, I'd like to thank my wife for supporting me in my crazy endeavors. She's been my everything and no amount of thanks will ever convey how deeply your love and support means to me.

About the Author

Jay Bower is a horror author living outside St. Louis, MO in the forest of Southern Illinois. He spends his time reading, writing, and convincing his wife the dark stories he writes do not involve her.

For links to all his books, visit his website. There you can also get a free story for signing up to his reader list.

jaybowerauthor.com

facebook.com/jaybowerauthor
x.com/JayBowerAuthor
instagram.com/jaybowerauthor
tiktok.com/@jaybowerauthor

ALSO BY JAY BOWER

Horror Novels

The Dark Sacrifice

Soul Eyes

Useless Creatures

Dreamwraith

Slaughter Lake (Co-written with David Viergutz)

Master of Demons

Cadaverous

The Brownsville Nightmares (Collects The Dark Sacrifice, Soul Eyes, and Dreamwraith)

Every Time I Die

The Terror of Willow Falls

Dead Blood Series

Dead Blood: Book One

Dead Blood: Book Two

Dead Blood: Book Three

Dead Blood: The Complete Series

Short Story Collections

Hanging Corpses

The Conservator's Collection: Derelict (with John Durgin and John Lynch)

9 798330 204205